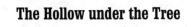

The Hollow under the Tree

The
Hollow
under the
Tree

Cary Fagan

Groundwood Books
House of Anansi Press
Toronto Berkeley

Groundwood Books / House of Anansi Press
groundwoodbooks.com

We acknowledge for their financial support of our publishing program the Canada
Council for the Arts, the Ontario Arts Council and the Government of Canada.

Library and Archives Canada Cataloguing in Publication
Fagan, Cary, author
The hollow under the tree / Cary Fagan.
Issued in print and electronic formats.
ISBN 978-1-55498-999-7 (hardcover).—ISBN 978-1-77306-000-2 (HTML).—
ISBN 978-1-77306-001-9 (Kindle)
I. Title.
PS8561.A375H65 2018   JC813'.54   C2017-905950-5
C2017-905951-3

Jacket art by Nolan Pelletier
Jacket design by Michael Solomon

Printed and bound in Canada

For my mother, Belle Fagan, with love

1

— ✳ —

Scaredy-Cat

A TRAIN approached the city from the west. The steam engine's giant wheels turned as smoke trailed behind, blacker than the night sky.

It was May 15, 1925. The train had pulled out of Buffalo, New York, fourteen hours late, due to a faulty hitch between the last two cars. A new hitch was supposed to arrive, but it never did. So the train's owner, Josiah Wasserman, insisted that the faulty one be welded together so that the circus could move on.

Josiah Wasserman was the proprietor of Wasserman's Spectacular Circus and Animal Menagerie. The performers had finished in Buffalo and were supposed to move on to Toronto. But because of the delay, Mr. Wasserman had decided to skip the city and head to the next destination, Montreal. The people of Toronto would be deprived of the Wasserman circus, with its acrobats, clowns, elephants, bears and other exotic beasts.

The stationmaster at Union Station had already been notified that the train would not stop. The steam engine did not need to slow down much as it approached. Most of the circus employees were asleep in their bunks. But the animals, which had been confined too long and had missed a feeding, whined and howled in their cages.

One employee couldn't sleep. His name was Sam Hibbins, the assistant animal trainer. He had once been the head trainer, but the owner felt that Sam was too soft on the animals, and so he demoted him. Besides, Sam was getting old.

Now he lay on a straw mattress that he had taken from his bunk, his dachshund Daisy beside him. He had placed the mattress beside a cage in the last car of the train. After this car there was only the caboose.

Sam never slept well anyway, but on this particular night he was worrying about the lion in the cage next to him. This male lion was the youngest of five owned by the Wasserman circus. He was just about grown, with a magnificent and nearly full mane, a handsome face and a powerfully muscular, if still slim, body.

He looked every inch the king of the beasts.

In fact, he was a scaredy-cat.

The lion had been born at the circus's winter home in Florida, only to be rejected by his mother. Sam had brought the tiny cub into his own bed to keep warm. He sang to him and held a baby's bottle to his hungry mouth.

The cub was a particularly sweet-natured animal, so Sam named him Sunshine, or Sunny. Not surprisingly, Sunny became attached to the old trainer — so attached that he wouldn't let another human come near. That included the lion tamer called Fearless Fotham, a sour-tempered man with a handlebar moustache and a drinking problem.

Sunny was even more afraid of other lions. When Sunny was old enough, Fearless Fotham brought him into the ring, cracking his whip over the young lion's head to make him rise up. But Sunny jumped off his stool in fear, banging into the mature male lion next to him, who bit Sunny on the ear.

Sunny howled. The other lions began to roar. Fearless Fotham smacked Sunny on the thigh with his club. Sunny dived to the ground, causing the lions on either side to snarl as they swiped at him with their claws. The scene might have ended in bloodshed if Sam Hibbins hadn't risked his own life by jumping into the ring and separating the lions with stern words. He led Sunny out of the ring while Fearless Fotham, cursing loudly, used his whip to keep the others in place.

This near-catastrophe happened in Buffalo, and it was the reason that Sunny was traveling in his own car. Josiah Wasserman was threatening to sell the animal to a zoo in Ohio. Sam didn't want Sunny to languish in some dismal cage for the rest of his life, so he asked for another chance. He had a bed for himself and Daisy in the same car so that the animal would stay calm.

As the train approached Toronto, Sam opened the car door to let in the early summer air. The dachshund yawned and shuddered in her sleep.

But the lion, poor creature, paced in the swaying cage, moaning unhappily.

What, thought Sam, was he going to do with Sunny?

Just then came the high whine of metal under stress, and then a sudden lurch.

"What the ...?" Sam said.

The faulty hitch had broken again.

— • —

THE TRAIN was less than ten miles from Toronto's downtown Union Station. The weld cracked, the hitch broke in two, and the last car, along with the caboose, was released from the rest of the train. The steam engine surged forward while the separated car and caboose began to slow down. The car tilted and the wheels jumped off the rails. It began to tip sideways, skidding on the gravel track and pulling the caboose over with it.

The terrified lion pawed the wooden floor, trying not to slide against the bars.

Sam Hibbins grabbed Daisy as they were thrown out of bed. Another jolt caused him to tumble head over heels, right out the open car door. He landed in some dense bushes that grew along the track. The bushes scratched him up but also cushioned his and Daisy's fall.

But the lion was trapped in the cage. The car began to slide down the slope of the track bed. Sunny was tossed sideways, banging his jaw against a bar. The cage twisted, buckled and split apart, sending splinters of metal and wood in every direction. The lion was thrown free of the debris. He landed in bushes a hundred yards farther on.

Sunny lay there for a minute or two before rising painfully, bruised on his thigh and shoulder and ribs. He shook himself and limped past the bits of wood and metal to begin walking up the dark hill ahead.

The lion came to a post in the ground. He smelled on it the disagreeable odor of the many dogs that had stopped there to lift their legs.

Attached to the post was a sign:

Welcome to High Park
No Littering

Of course, Sunny couldn't read, but he could smell earth, trees, grass, wildflowers, water.

He limped on.

2

The Pie Maker's Daughter

"I HATE the way he watches me from the window," Sadie Menken said to her father. Strawberries had just come into season, and he was pouring the red filling into the pie crusts while Sadie evened it out with a spatula.

"He goes from one window to another," Sadie went on. "Sometimes he holds things up. Yesterday it was some dumb hand puppet. Or he makes faces. Maybe next time I'll bring a rotten tomato with me. Then I'll throw it at the window — *splat!* That would show him."

"Maybe he's curious about you," her father said. He put a flattened circle of dough over a filled pie, trimmed it and began to pinch the edges.

When they had finished, twenty-five pies were lined up on the wooden table waiting to be baked.

"Maybe he's lonely and wants a friend," her father went on, picking up a pie with each hand while opening the heavy oven door with his foot. "Rich people can be lonely, too."

Sadie pretended to choke herself and then fell to the ground, gagging. When her father merely continued to work, she got up again.

"And you could use a friend," her father said.

"I'm too busy. I have … *responsibilities*." She used her most adult voice.

"I know you do. Too many, in fact. You need to have some fun. But you'd better be off or you'll be late for school."

"Oh, don't worry. I'm sure the school wouldn't dare to start before I got there."

"You sound awfully important," her father said with a smile.

"You have no idea how important I am in that place. And how popular. Why, I'm the *most* popular person in school. It just can't run without me."

With that, Sadie turned around and headed to the front hall to pick up her satchel.

SADIE AND HER father lived in a small house on Radford Avenue, just a few blocks from High Park. In 1925, Toronto was a city of horse-drawn wagons and rickety streetcars and noisy Model T Fords. Electrical wires crossed overhead from pole to pole like spiderwebs. It was a city of red brick and gray stone and small houses lined in rows, but big houses, too. There were hotels and movie palaces and department stores and factories with tall chimneys spewing smoke. Boys wore knee-length breeches, and girls wore dresses.

Even Sadie Menken, who liked to spend her time catching frogs and climbing trees, wore a dress and stockings and well-shined shoes.

To Sadie, High Park was the best thing about the city. It was so big, it was almost a country of its own. It was part valley, part forest and part plains. Here and there were clearings for a playground, a garden, a picnic area, a tennis court. Small streams trickled south down the slope towards Grenadier Pond at the bottom. Sadie would have spent all her time in the park after school, if she didn't have to deliver pies.

There are many stories about children without a mother or a father or both. A reader might think that every child in the world was an orphan! And yet here is another, for Sadie Menken had lost her own mother. That was how her father put it. Lost.

But she wasn't dead. Instead, she had left them for the dream of becoming a Broadway actress in New York. She hadn't yet become a big star, but she hadn't come back, either. Sadie could barely remember her.

Sadie loved her father and only wished that he wasn't so busy. As a pie maker he had to get up at five in the morning to begin rolling out the dough and warming up the ovens. By the time Sadie got up he had already finished his first batch. He made pies in many varieties, depending on the fruit in season — rhubarb, strawberry, cherry, peach, plum, blueberry, apple. His pies were delicious, and he had a standing order from the King Edward Hotel as well as several restaurants and private homes.

He would bake all day, pausing only to make dinner, after which he would spend an hour preparing for the next day before falling into bed, exhausted.

Sadie knew how hard her father worked. When she was little she would keep him company, sitting on a stool and chatting as she played with a ball of dough. But as she got older she began to help. Now she could roll out the dough, cut up the fruit, make the cross-hatches in the top of the pie to let out the steam as it baked.

But her main job happened after school. Every day she delivered six or eight pies to houses in the neighborhood. She had an old Red Bird delivery bicycle with a square iron basket between the handlebars where the pie boxes could be stacked. Although she was small, Sadie had grown used to pedaling the heavy bicycle and keeping it steady, so as not to damage the pies.

Her route took her through the nearby streets where the grandest houses stood, lived in by rich bankers and businessmen. The last pie always went to the house of Mr. Theodore Kendrick, whose handsome stone residence stood on a rise just one block from the park.

It was in this house that a boy always stood in an upper window watching Sadie as she climbed off her bicycle. The same boy she had complained to her father about. He would scurry from one window to another to see her better as she carried the pie box through the open gate, past the front door and around to the servants' entrance. There she would knock on the door and wait for the maid. The boy would look through the nearest window and wave his fingers at her. He had a round face and bangs and to Sadie looked like a smiling pie plate.

On this afternoon, Sadie passed through the Kendricks' gate as usual, went around to the side door and banged the knocker. Sure enough, the boy appeared, only this time he looked at her through a brass spyglass. She waited and knocked again.

At last the door opened to reveal not the maid, but the boy himself. He was wearing a blue and white sailor suit, complete with little hat and ribbon.

"Good afternoon," he said. "I'm Theodore Kendrick Junior. But everyone calls me Theo Junior."

"And I'm one of Santa's elves."

"You're the pie maker's daughter."

"You're the bee's knees in that outfit."

"You think so?"

"Of course not. You look ridiculous."

Perhaps another boy might have shown that his feelings were hurt, but Theo Junior just looked at Sadie thoughtfully. "I wasn't sure. My mother sent it by steamship from Paris."

"Here's your pie," Sadie said. "Be careful. If you drop it you still have to pay."

"I'm sure it's scrumptious," Theodore Junior said. "They always are."

"All this pie," Sadie said, "is making you fat."

"I'm naturally round. It runs in the family. My father says that we're 'robust.' But I do have an exercise trainer. And I have a cello instructor and an astronomy teacher and —"

But Sadie had already turned around. She marched to her bicycle and rode back the way she had come.

Perhaps the boy's feelings *were* hurt. Whose wouldn't be?

3

❋

Blue

BUT THE next day, the boy answered the door again. This time he was wearing a flying-ace outfit complete with pilot's jacket, leather helmet and goggles. The goggles, thought Sadie, made him look like a frog.

"Up, up and away!" Theodore Junior said, making his hand into an airplane taking off.

"If you say so. Here's your pie."

"I hope it's blueberry."

"Blueberries aren't in season. But I suppose a pilot wouldn't know that because he has his head in the clouds."

"That's a good one. So what kind is it?"

"Snotberry."

"Snotberry? Never heard of it. Are snotberries *green*?"

Sadie almost smiled. "Maybe."

"Because I really do have a *nose* for pie."

"I'm sorry I started this," Sadie said, turning away so he wouldn't see her laugh.

"Goodbye!" he called, following her to her bicycle. "See you in the funny papers!"

Pedaling away, Sadie had to admit that Theodore Junior was a good sport. He didn't get mad at being teased the way most kids did. Otherwise, he was still annoying.

Thinking about Theodore Junior, she forgot to pay attention to the direction she was going. She steered her bicycle around the corner and down the alley.

And that was when she found her way blocked by three boys.

Sadie knew who they were. The Parkside Gang.

The Parkside Gang consisted of just three. Big Fergus Gumpy, who always wore a dirty cap pulled low over his eyes. And the Tarpinsky twins. Dylan and Wylie Tarpinsky were both pale and skinny, like two sheets of paper.

The three of them were carrying fishing rods made out of willow branches. They were probably on the way back from Grenadier Pond, where it looked like they'd had no luck. But Fergus was also carrying something else. A metal can of blue paint. Sadie knew it was blue because the top was missing and some of the paint had sloshed over the sides.

"If it isn't that phonus balonus, Sadie Menken," said Fergus.

The three boys went to Sadie's school. She knew them well enough to be slightly nervous, even though she had always bluffed her way past them.

"Something smells fishy," she said. "And since you didn't catch anything, I guess it must be you."

"Shut your trap," hissed Fergus. "We don't care about fish because we found ourselves something better. A whole can of paint. From somebody's back porch."

"You mean you stole it."

Fergus shrugged. "How come you never give us one of your father's pies? You know I told you to."

"I thought about it. But then I decided it would be a waste of a good pie."

"You think you're so hotsy-totsy. Maybe we ought to teach you a lesson."

"Or I could teach you one," said Sadie. "Like how to tie your shoe."

Fergus looked down. Indeed, his shoelace was dragging.

"I like it that way."

"What are you going to do with the paint? Pour it over your head?"

As soon as the words were out of her mouth, Sadie knew she had gone too far.

Fergus's wide mouth turned up into a grin.

"That's not a bad idea," he said.

"I was just making a joke." Sadie took a step back.

Fergus nodded at the twins. They dashed forward and grabbed Sadie by the arms. She kicked at the twins and struggled to get free, but they held her tight. Fergus came forward and because he was so much bigger, it was easy for him to lift the paint can high. Slowly he tipped it forward, the thick paint dripping onto Sadie's head and down her face and neck. She closed her eyes and held her breath even as she pulled this way and that.

"Hey, you're splashing us!" Wylie said.

The twins let go. She wiped the paint from her nose and mouth and gasped for air. She hardly noticed the sound of the Parkside Gang as they ran away, whooping and hollering.

She stood there as the paint continued to slide down, all the way to her shoes.

There was nothing for Sadie to do but walk the rest of the way home. She found some old newspaper and wiped off as much of the paint as she could. She wrapped some paper around the bicycle handles and pulled it along, leaving blue footprints behind her.

At her own back door, she made sure nobody was around before pulling off her shoes and dress and stockings. Then she ran into the house, hurrying up the stairs.

"Is that you, Sadie?" her father called from the kitchen.

"I'm going to take a bath!"

"Really? That will be the first time I don't have to remind you."

It took her a long time to get all the blue off, using a stiff brush and a cake of pumice soap. Her skin felt raw from the scrubbing, but she was clean.

Before that day, blue had been Sadie's favorite color.

But it never was again.

4

— ✳ —

The News

MISS MARJORIE Clemons was a boarder living in the Menken house. She was an older woman with orange hair who wore an impressive array of necklaces and bracelets that jangled when she moved. Miss Clemons had worked for almost forty years in a library in Lambeth in "dear old England," as she called it. Upon retiring, she was convinced by her best friend, a widow named Abigail Foster, to immigrate to Canada so that the two would be company for each other.

Miss Clemons had a series of oak filing cabinets lining her bedroom, the largest in the house.

She spent a considerable portion of each day reading newspapers and clipping articles that interested her. She would then file them according to her own categories, such as *People Rescued out of Holes, Remarkable Explosions* and *Unusual Animals Found in Hat Boxes.*

And so for the past three years, Miss Clemons had eaten her suppers at the Menken table and read her newspapers, scissors on her capacious lap, in the Menken sitting room.

At first Sadie had resented this intruder in the house, replying to her questions with rude grunts, staring resentfully whenever she took a second helping of roasted potatoes.

But like all good librarians, Miss Clemons was a patient woman. One evening when Sadie was having trouble with a school project on the Panama Canal, Miss Clemons retrieved several useful articles from her archives. On another occasion, when Sadie tangled up the scarf she was trying to knit for home economics, Miss Clemons gently took the needles from her hands and sorted it out.

It was at the supper table, several days after Sadie's encounter with the Parkside Gang, that Miss Clemons said, "I have clipped out a very interesting article from the newspaper today."

"What would we do if you didn't keep us up to date?" Sadie's father said.

"No doubt you would remain sadly ignorant of current affairs," Miss Clemons answered. She cleared her throat and began to read.

A Canine Conundrum

Residents of the High Park neighborhood have reported the disappearance of several dogs in the past two weeks.

Local shoe-store owner Herman Spudnik said, "Our Patches always liked to ramble after dark. He's a cocker spaniel, you see. But the other night he went out and didn't come back. We've looked everywhere but he seems to have vanished."

Besides the missing dogs, several people strolling in the park have come across squirrel tails. "We hope that children aren't up to mischief," said Mrs. Louise Frost, who lives north of the park. "Offering peanuts to the squirrels and then snipping off their tails!"

So far the police are showing little interest in these strange events. "We've got actual crimes to worry about," said Sergeant Jaworski. "Just the other day somebody painted blue footprints along the sidewalk. That's defacement of public property."

Miss Clemons put down the article. "In my opinion there are far too many dogs in the city. Still, people do get attached to their pets. My friend Abigail's lap-dog, Lucretia, is very dear to her."

Mr. Menken nodded, although Sadie saw that he was only half-listening. No doubt he was mentally counting the number of pies he needed to make for the next day's orders. But Sadie had listened to every word.

Of course, the reference to blue footprints made her blush.

But she found something else far more interesting.

She remembered another newspaper article that Miss Clemons had read to them not long ago. It was about a circus train that had been traveling on the railway tracks below High Park when some cars had broken away and crashed. At first it was feared that a man had been killed, but he had been found wandering about with a large bump on his head. The newspaper said that only a young lion had been lost.

Miss Clemons had assumed that "lost" meant dead. So did every other reader. But Sadie had learned to say that she had lost her mother even though her mother was living in New York City.

What if the lion wasn't dead, either?

What if "lost" just meant that it had never been found?

5

— ✳ —

The Hollow Tree

ON SATURDAY, Sadie had an idea.

Her father quit baking early on Saturdays. He was taking his last batch out of the oven while she folded boxes at the table.

"Looks like I've got a broken one. It's honey rhubarb. Want a piece?"

A broken pie had a crust that had cracked or caved in during baking. It tasted just as good, but customers wanted pies that looked perfect. There was usually one every day or two, and Sadie got more than her share. She may have been the only person in Toronto who wasn't eager for a piece of Menken's homemade pie.

"No, thanks," she said. "But I do know somebody who'd like it."

"Take it."

Sadie slipped the pie into a box.

"I'll be home in time for dinner," she said. She picked up the pie, went out the front door, walked up to Bloor Street, turned right and went into Hathway's Butcher Shop.

Sadie never liked the smell of blood, but she did like the tinkle of the bell as she walked in, and she liked to slide on the sawdust sprinkled on the wooden floor. Behind the counter, Mr. Hathway was packaging up a string of sausages.

"Hi, Sadie, how's by you?"

"Everything's good, Mr. Hathway. I want to make a trade with you."

"One minute while I put away this knife. I wouldn't want to get so distracted that I cut off my own finger."

Butchers sure had a weird sense of humor, thought Sadie.

"I want to trade you one of my dad's pies."

"A Menken pie? You bet. What do you want for it? I'm a pretty tough negotiator, you know."

"It's honey rhubarb."

"Honey rhubarb? Sweet *and* tart. You can have the whole store!"

"I don't want the whole store. I just need a bunch

of — what's the word? Scraps, I guess. You see, I've been feeding some cats."

"Cats, you say. How many?"

Sadie tried to imagine how many ordinary cats might fit into one very large one.

"Twenty?"

"That's a lot of cats! But you're in luck. I've got a pile of stuff in the refrigerator. I'll make you up a nice package."

— • —

A RED STREETCAR rattled by as Sadie came out of the shop. A shout made her look up.

Fergus Gumpy and the Tarpinsky twins were hanging onto the back of the streetcar as it moved along. They had jumped on without paying.

Fergus waved his cap. "What's wrong, Sadie? Feeling kind of *blue*?"

Sadie wasn't scared of much, yet the sight of those grinning boys made her breath come quick. But by the time she yelled out, "Don't fall off, you'll hurt the road!" the streetcar was already grinding its way around the corner. It was a lame comeback anyway, she thought.

Sadie went through the east gate of High Park, not far from her own house. She turned away from the popular picnic tables and playgrounds and onto a side path, following it down to Grenadier Pond. When she was little, her father used to take her to feed the ducks, and then to the small zoo to see the mountain goats in their pens and the peacocks that wandered freely through the park.

She moved off the path and made her way between trees and bushes, around small hills and across tinkling streams. She shifted the parcel to her other arm.

Where would I hide from people? Sadie asked herself. She stared hard at piles of leaves, mounds of rock. She even looked up into the tree branches.

After a while she came to a small grassy circle. The parcel felt heavy. She sat down, feeling tired and discouraged. Her eyes began to close.

She heard a noise.

Sadie's eyes opened. In front of her was a dark hollow topped by an enormous tangle of roots. The roots belonged to a giant old maple tree that had toppled over. She looked at its blackened branches and realized that the tree had been struck by lightning. It had died and the roots must have pulled up out of the earth when it fell, leaving a space beneath.

A space almost like a cave.

Sadie stood up. She took a step closer and peered into the dark of the hollow.

At first she couldn't see anything.

Then two yellow eyes appeared in the dark. They stared at her.

Sadie didn't move. Her legs wanted to run, but her shoes felt glued to the ground.

The yellow eyes blinked. And then came a flash of light — teeth! — and a low moan.

Her heart beat fast. The parcel! She lowered it to the ground and fumbled to untie the string. She folded back the paper, showing the glistening scraps inside. The smell of raw meat rose up.

A snarl made her jump with a cry. She took three cautious steps back.

The eyes didn't move.

"Hey, there," Sadie said, keeping her voice soft. "Are you hungry? I bet you are. Look, I brought you a nice snack. Why don't you come out and have a taste? Of Mr. Hathway's meat, I mean."

The eyes came towards her, and the lion — for it really was a lion — emerged from the hollow.

He wasn't just big the way Sadie had imagined. He was *huge*. Sadie took two more steps back, even though she knew that if the lion pounced, there was no chance she could get away.

He had a beautiful face with a soft-looking triangular nose and long whiskers and a big mane. As he stepped forward, she could see the muscles moving beneath his fur. His paws were almost the size of dinner plates. Yet he also looked thin — she could see his ribs.

Poor thing, she thought. He's half starved. Maybe it isn't enough to catch the occasional beagle or squirrel.

The lion stood on the grass, his tail swishing back and forth. He looked at her with an expression that seemed tremendously sad.

Sadie took another step back.

"Go on," she said. The lion looked at her another moment and then stepped forward, lowering his head. He began to gulp down the scraps. He was a messy eater. A noisy one, too. He ate every last morsel.

He even ate the paper.

"I hope you don't get a stomachache," Sadie said.

The lion looked up at her and licked his whiskers with a big pink tongue.

He belched.

Sadie giggled.

He roared.

Sadie ran.

6

A Good Listener

SADIE RAN all the way home and then halted on the front porch to compose herself before going inside. She spent the rest of that day, and all night, and the next day (which was Sunday) holding the secret inside her. It felt like a flame warming her insides.

On Monday she went to school, came home again to deliver pies (not even taking the time to tease Theodore Junior), and took a broken one to Mr. Hathway in the butcher shop. When she got to the park, she went straight to the clearing, checking to make sure that nobody saw where she was going.

She put the package down and untied it. Then she stepped back, only not quite so far.

The yellow eyes appeared and the lion stepped out of the hollow, looking even bigger and more beautiful. He ate all the meat, this time leaving the paper. Then he turned and walked back into the dark.

Sadie grabbed up the paper and sprinted home again.

And so began her afternoon routine. She couldn't go every day because once in a while there were no broken pies to trade, or her father fell behind in his orders and asked her to come straight back from her deliveries to help him in the kitchen. But she went as often as she could, and it wasn't long before the lion began to expect her.

One late afternoon Sadie was kneeling on the grass, struggling to undo a stubborn knot in the string that held together the package of meat. She had just got it undone when a large impatient nose nudged her shoulder. She fell back with a shriek, scaring the lion, who bounded back into his hollow.

She caught her breath and called softly to the lion. But it took several minutes to coax him out again. After he had finished eating, he surprised her by flopping down on the ground and cleaning himself with his tongue like a big house cat. Sadie got to look at him closely.

Was his fur soft or rough? It looked soft. Perhaps he lay down because he wanted her company. She took one step forward, then another and sat cross-legged on the ground. She told the lion about her house, and her father, and Miss Clemons and the Parkside Gang. She even told him about her mother and the memory she had of her practicing the one line she had in an upcoming play. *I see nothing funny about it, I see nothing funny about it*, her mother had said over and over until Sadie couldn't stop laughing. She hadn't told that to anyone before, not even her father.

The lion was a good listener, gazing off into the distance when he wasn't licking his fur or biting at some itchy spot on his flank. After a while he closed his eyes. And when Sadie ran out of things to say, she found herself getting sleepy, too.

Her own eyes closed. She slept.

When she woke, she found herself leaning against the lion's warm side, feeling his slow breathing.

A sound woke the lion. He rose to his feet, almost knocking Sadie over, and bounded back into the hollow.

"One kiss wouldn't hurt!"

"You're going to have to catch me!"

A woman giggled and began to run through the woods, followed by a man. They made an awful lot of noise, but Sadie could hear them moving away until the clearing was silent again. Looking into the hollow, she saw the animal's yellow eyes blink at her.

"You're right to keep away from people," Sadie said. "They can be awfully stupid."

The lion belched.

"Good one," Sadie said, turning to go home.

7

— ✳ —

Feathers

SADIE DROPPED a pie box onto the butcher-shop counter.

"Hey, Mr. Hathway. I've got one of your favorites today. Apple crumble."

Mr. Hathway smacked down a cleaver, cutting a rack of ribs in half.

"I'm sorry, Sadie, but Mrs. Hathway has nixed any more pies for a while. She thinks I don't like her baking anymore. Just between you and me, your father's is better. Besides, there's a man who wants to buy all my scraps. He's making canned food for dogs, if you can believe it. I hope you'll find another way to feed your cats."

"Okay, Mr. Hathway. Thanks, anyway."

Sadie's heart sank as she left the shop. The lion hadn't eaten since the day before yesterday. She decided to visit him anyway, and just in case she put down the pie box with the lid open. But it turned out that lions didn't like pie, not even apple crumble.

The lion sniffed it and looked at Sadie as if to say, Is that all you've got? He gave a mournful whine, but he still must have been glad to see her, for he lay on the grass. Sadie was close enough to hear a low, continuous rumble.

"Hey, you're purring," Sadie said. "Don't worry. I'll find you something to eat."

— • —

THE NEXT DAY Miss Clemons brought another newspaper clipping to the supper table.

"This is quite shocking," she said as she began to read.

Peacock Meets Violent End

Yesterday morning a mother pushing her carriage in High Park came upon a strange sight. In the middle of the path was a heap of brilliant feathers — feathers that could only have belonged to one of the park's beloved peacocks. Remembering the previous disappearance of several neighborhood dogs, the woman returned to the street to fetch a constable.

"This is a criminal act," said Sergeant Jaworski after he personally viewed the remains of the exotic bird. "That peacock was city property."

"I know how you like to wander in the park, young Sadie," said Miss Clemons. "But it isn't safe, not while there is a murderer of peacocks out there."

Mr. Menken picked up a knife to carve the roast chicken. Sadie wished that she could get some of it for the lion, but she knew that her father needed to stretch their budget and would use the remains to make soup or a chicken pot pie.

"Miss Clemons is right, Sadie. You have to be careful."

"Maybe something in the park was hungry. After all, we eat birds, too." Sadie pointed to the platter. "What's the difference?"

Her father looked at the chicken. "About fifty dollars, I should think."

As if it wasn't bad enough that she couldn't find food, now the police were becoming interested. But what could she do? She thought about the lion for the rest of the evening. She had trouble falling asleep, and found it on her mind when she woke up in the morning. As always, she helped get breakfast on the table and cleared the dishes afterwards, went to school and came home again to make her deliveries.

She wasn't much in the mood for Theodore Junior, but there he was at the back door. He wore a black tuxedo with a bow tie and a silk hankie in the pocket and even a top hat.

"You going to start tap dancing?" Sadie said.

"It's for our family trip to Europe. On an ocean liner. I have to dress for dinner."

"Any chance you're leaving soon?"

"Not for a couple of months. I'm trying to get used to the outfit." He took the box from her. "So what kind of pie is it today?"

"I didn't notice. You want me to stick my thumb in and see?"

"That depends. Is your thumb clean or dirty?"

Sadie was in no mood to joke. She turned to go. But then an idea made her stop.

"So, tell me, Theo Junior. Do you know what you're having for dinner?"

"Sure. Big, juicy T-bone steaks."

"You wouldn't by any chance want to give them to me?"

"You're a funny egg. I can never tell when you're joking."

"I'm not joking."

Theodore Junior looked at her seriously.

"I guess so," he said finally. "Cook won't be very happy, but I'll tell her I have a craving for spaghetti."

He took the pie into the house while Sadie waited. If there was a slower boy on earth than Theo Junior she had never met him. But at last he came back with a package wrapped in butcher's paper closed not by string like Mr. Hathway's but with a gold seal.

"That's great."

"It must be hard when your family can't afford to buy food."

"It isn't for my family! Maybe we don't have steaks but we still eat."

Sadie reached out for the parcel, but Theo Junior pulled it away.

"If it's not for your family, what do you want it for?"

"It's for a friend."

"Your friend must be awfully hungry."

"He's got a big appetite."

"I'd like to meet this friend."

"Trust me, you don't want to. Besides, you might get in trouble."

"I've never been in trouble before. I'm interested to know what it feels like."

Could Sadie risk taking him? His interested expression was annoying, but it wasn't mean or sneaky.

"All right. You can come with me."

"Great. I just have to change out of my tuxedo."

"You're going to make me wait again?"

But Sadie did wait, and when Theo Junior came back in his everyday clothes, she made him carry the parcel of steaks. It took hardly any time to walk to the east gate of the park.

"Are we going into High Park?" asked Theo Junior. "I've always wanted to see what it was like."

"You've never been in the park? What a bunch of malarkey."

"Is it like the Tuileries Garden in Paris or Hyde Park in London? I've been to them. Hey, look at those swings! Want to go on?"

"We're on a mission here, Theo Junior."

"Just for a minute. Please."

"Fine. Get on and I'll push."

So Theodore Junior climbed up on the worn wooden seat of the swing, and Sadie got behind and pushed him.

"Not too high!" he cried, but Sadie just pushed harder.

"You get on one, too."

It had been a long time since she'd played in the park. When she wasn't in school she was helping her father in the kitchen or delivering pies or doing homework. So she got on the swing next to Theodore Junior and pumped her legs hard to catch up.

"Hey, I forgot how fun this is," she said.

"I didn't even know how fun this is!"

But five minutes later she insisted that they start walking again. They turned off the path, through the wooded area and into the clearing.

"This is a nice spot," Theo Junior said. "Are we going to make a fire and cook the steaks for your friend?"

"Not exactly." She took the parcel from him and put it on the ground, tearing off the seal so that she could spread open the paper. Then she stepped back.

"I don't get it," Theo Junior said.

"*Sssh!* Your voice will spook him."

"Spook who?"

She knelt down. "That's okay, you can come out. Come and get your dinner."

"Is somebody in there? But, Sadie, you can't possibly know somebody who lives under a —"

Theo Junior stopped talking. He stopped because two yellow eyes had just appeared in the dark. The eyes grew larger and then a soft nose became visible, and the lion stepped into the late afternoon light.

"What?" said Theo Junior. "*What?*"

The lion padded up to the parcel and licked the top steak. He let out a sigh as he lay down, pulling the T-bone between his paws.

"Ah, ah, ah …" said Theo Junior, his eyes as wide as silver dollars.

"Go on, lion. I know you're hungry. See, Theo Junior? He likes your steaks. Theo?"

47

Sadie turned but Theo Junior was gone. Then she heard the sound of a branch cracking and looked up.

Theo Junior was in a tree. He had climbed impressively high.

"You really can come down," she said. "Anyway, I think lions can climb trees."

Slowly he came down again and stood beside her.

"That's a real live lion, Sadie."

"Yup."

"In High Park. A lion living in High Park."

"Say something nice to him. You have to make friends."

Theo Junior cleared his throat. "I'm pleased to make your acquaintance."

The lion paid no attention. Instead, he began to tear the meat from the last steak. When he had finished the meat, he began to crunch on the bone.

"Where did you get him?"

"I didn't get him. I found him."

"Well, it must be finders keepers. Sadie's lion." He repeated the words. "Sadie's lion."

Sadie rubbed her chin. Was the lion really hers? The animal picked up the remains of the bones with his teeth and trotted back into the hollow. They couldn't see him, but they could hear him gnawing away.

"He'll go to sleep soon," Sadie said. "He likes to nap after dinner."

"This is amazing, Sadie. This is stupendous! I can't wait to tell my friend. Wait, I don't have a friend. Wait till I tell the cook —"

Sadie grabbed his arm.

"No, no, no. Absolutely not. You can't tell anyone. Not unless you want me to be sorry I brought you."

8

— ✳ —

Manners

ON THE way home, Theo Junior found that he was trembling. He even held out a shaking hand. Sadie was more interested in explaining exactly why he couldn't tell anybody about the lion. People would panic. The Parkside Gang might come with rocks and sticks. The police might even shoot him.

"What's the Parkside Gang?" Theo Junior asked.

"Never mind. Do you get my point?"

"Sure. But a lion can't stay in the park forever. Somebody is bound to see him. Or he might get scared and eat, er, bite someone. You know, by accident."

"We have to figure something out. But until we

do we'll have to feed him so he won't eat any more animals and attract attention."

Sadie stopped in front of her house.

"Is this where you live?" Theo Junior said. "It's so small."

"It used to be bigger, but it shrank in the rain."

"That's funny. But I meant it in a nice way. It looks cozy."

"I'll see you tomorrow. You'll get more meat?"

"I can ask Cook to put in an extra order. You know, Sadie, it *is* supper time about now."

"So?"

"So it's been a common practice since ancient times to invite a hungry traveler to share your meal."

"You're not a traveler. You live three blocks away. Besides, won't your parents be expecting you?"

"They're spending a month in Bar Harbor, wherever that is. So it's only the cook and the maid and the chauffeur. I can telephone and tell them. I mean, if you invite me."

"You're awfully pushy," Sadie said. But she let Theo Junior follow her inside. Most houses in the city didn't have telephones, but her father needed one to receive his orders. Theo Junior telephoned home and then they washed their hands and joined Miss Clemons at the dining-room table.

"And who is this boy you've brought home?" Miss Clemons asked as she tucked her napkin onto her lap.

"My name is Theodore Kendrick Junior and I am pleased to make your acquaintance."

"Such fine manners! Young man, your expressive eyes remind me of the great opera singer Feodor Chaliapin. Do you see this young gentleman, Mr. Menken?"

"I certainly do," said Sadie's father, coming in with a cast-iron pot. "And we're glad to have you with us, Theodore."

"Just a moment," said Miss Clemons. "Did you say Kendrick? Of the Kendrick Oatmeal Porridge fortune?"

"Yes, ma'am, that's us."

"Dear Sadie, I had no idea that you hobnobbed with such high society."

"Neither did I," said Sadie. "What's for supper?"

"Monday's leftover stew, I'm afraid," said her father. "I had a last-minute order from the King Edward Hotel for twenty pies."

"I think stew tastes even better the next day," said Theo Junior. "At least, I imagine it does."

Miss Clemons questioned Theo Junior about his family, about whom she had often read in the society columns. Sadie found the conversation very dull. Theo Junior had proved himself useful as a source of meat, and it had felt good to tell her secret to somebody. But could she count on him to keep it to himself?

Not long after supper was over, the doorbell rang.

"That's good old Grierson, who's come to pick me up," said Theo Junior. "Mr. Menken, thank you for having me in your lovely home. Miss Clemons, it was delightful to meet someone as interesting as you."

"Feodor Chaliapin! You have the very same manners. If only you had his bass singing voice. But you certainly must come back," Miss Clemons said.

"I will if I'm invited."

Sadie rolled her eyes. She walked with him out to the porch. The chauffeur stood by the Lincoln limousine at the curb. It was the biggest car she had ever seen, with shiny black fenders and square windows and round silver headlights.

"You sure know how to butter up the adults. Now get into your jalopy and go home. And don't forget to bring the meat tomorrow."

"I won't. This is the most exciting thing that has ever happened to me."

"Remember, you can't tell anyone."

"You're not very good at trusting people."

And with those words, Theo Junior skipped down the steps and ducked into the back of the limousine. The chauffeur shut the door, got into the front and drove away. Sadie guessed that it would take them about one and a half minutes to reach their house.

9

Monster

THE NEXT DAY, Theo Junior met Sadie at the entrance to the park, a parcel of ground sirloin in his leather satchel. And the day after, and the day after that. He grew easier around the lion, although he still kept a step or two behind Sadie.

"I prefer to observe wildlife from a respectful distance," he said.

"Applesauce! You keep behind me so that if the lion pounces, he'll eat me first."

The lion clearly enjoyed the high quality of his suppers. After eating he would lie on the grass, cleaning his fur or just sitting with half-closed eyes and purring. The sound reminded Theo Junior of a small motor boat.

Sadie noticed that the animal's ribs didn't show as much. His eyes shone and his fur looked thicker.

May turned into June and each day seemed more beautiful than the last. Sadie felt as if the world was brighter and clearer than it had ever been. The lion came out of the hollow eagerly now, and once when Theo Junior was unwrapping the parcel, he felt a rough tongue on the back of his hand. He couldn't speak for five minutes afterwards.

— • —

"WHERE ARE my reading glasses?" Miss Clemons said one night at dinner. "Ah, here they are, right on my nose. I must read you this distressing newspaper article. It seems our city is inhabited by a monster."

"A monster?" said Sadie's father, serving the fried fish. "How exciting."

Theo Junior and Sadie looked at one another. Theo often ate supper at the Menken table these days.

Miss Clemons began to read..

Police Pursue Peril in Park

Last night a gentleman made a startling report to the Toronto Police. He had been strolling in High Park just after dusk when a terrible beast leapt out at him.

"We had gone off the path," said Herbert Biswith, a veteran of the Great War. "I picked up a stone and threw it into the dark. Just for fun, you see. A moment later this monster leapt out of nowhere. It had huge burning eyes and spikes around its head and teeth as large as butcher knives. I've never been so terrified, not even in battle. It clamped its teeth on the brim of my new hat. I turned and ran as fast as I could."

It seems that even the police can no longer ignore these strange events in High Park.

"We are taking immediate action," said Sergeant Jaworski. "We will do a complete search of the park. We will look under every rock and behind every tree. If there is a monster, we will find it. And rest assured, we will make sure it disturbs the good citizens of Toronto no more."

Miss Clemons took off her reading glasses.

"It's about time, I say. Sometimes I think it's no longer safe to walk in this city. If I were you, Mr. Menken, I wouldn't let Sadie go into the park until this is settled."

Sadie's father served the green beans and mashed potatoes. "My Sadie is a smart girl. She knows to keep out of trouble. Still, it probably is a good idea to stay out of the park for the time being."

Sadie kept her eyes on her plate. She no longer had much appetite, and only wanted to talk alone with Theo Junior. But she had to wait until her father asked her to clear the plates and make tea and serve everyone a piece of broken peach pie.

"What are we going to do?" Theo Junior asked as they waited on the porch for the chauffeur. "They'll find the hollow. And the lion in it."

"Can you meet me here at midnight?"

"Your father said you shouldn't go into the park."

The black limousine pulled up to the curb.

"He said it was probably a good idea not to, but he didn't forbid me. Will you come?"

And even before he spoke, Sadie knew what Theo Junior's answer would be.

— • —

NINETY YEARS AGO, when these events occurred, parents didn't worry so much about children being outside on their own. From a young age they walked to school alone and visited friends or went to the store to fetch a tin of baking powder or a spool of thread.

But even then, children were not supposed to be out at midnight.

Sadie did feel bad about deceiving her father, but she couldn't see any other way. She lay in bed, already dressed, and waited for the grandfather clock in the hall to strike twelve. Then she grabbed her jacket and her canvas knapsack, and crept out of the house.

Standing on the dark porch, she heard a rustling sound and saw something emerge from the bushes.

"Psst!"

Sadie jumped.

"Is that you, Sadie?"

"No, it's Charlie Chaplin."

Theodore Junior stepped up onto the porch. He turned on a flashlight and the beam hit Sadie's eyes.

"Point that thing somewhere else," she said. Theo Junior pointed it at himself. He was wearing a white pith helmet, a vest with a dozen pockets, short pants and hiking boots. He held a butterfly net in his other hand.

"What are you supposed to be?"

"My parents bought this outfit at the natural history museum in New York City. I'm supposed to look like Stanley, or maybe Livingstone."

"Never mind, let's go. And turn off the flashlight. Somebody might see it."

They walked silently to the park. At night the trees became dark and twisted forms, and the farther off the path they went, the less they could see.

"Stay close," said Theo Junior. "I, uh, don't want you to get scared."

"It's too late for that."

A few moments later they stepped into the clearing. The moon cast a silvery light on the grass and the tangled roots above the hollow.

"Hey, lion," Sadie called softly. "Come on out."

There was no sound. No yellow eyes.

"Lion?"

Theo Junior turned on his flashlight. He pointed it into the hollow.

It was empty.

"How are we going to find him?" Sadie asked. "We have to get him out of here before the police search the park."

"Maybe," Theo Junior said, looking behind her. "Maybe he'll find us."

Sadie turned around. And there was the lion, his head tilted to one side as if he was wondering what they were doing.

Theo Junior took a step backwards, but Sadie just wagged her finger. "No more games, now. Lie down. That's it. Lie down."

The lion shook his mane and sank to his knees.

"Did he just do what you asked?" Theo Junior said in wonder.

"Well, he *is* a circus lion." She took off her knapsack and pulled out a leather belt and a rope. "I borrowed this from my father."

"Sadie, you're not going to —"

But she did. She stepped up to the lion, draped the belt over his wide neck and buckled it under his chin.

"There," she said. "A nice collar. Not too tight. And this skipping rope will do for a leash."

"Really? A collar and leash?"

"How else will we get him out of here? You know we're your friends, don't you, lion? Let's go for a little walk."

Sadie moved away, the rope growing taut behind her. It was about eight feet long and stretched out until she was tugging on the collar.

The lion just looked at her.

"Come on," Sadie said. "Walk!"

And the lion did. Theo hurried to catch up.

"By the way, where are we going?"

"To your house."

"Excuse me?"

"Where do you think we should go, the Broadview Hotel? You have a garage in back. I've seen it."

"Yes, but the car usually goes in there."

"I guess you'd better make sure it doesn't. Now let's get a move on."

It was very late. Shops and restaurants were closed. Houses were dark. When a lone milk wagon passed, they hid behind a fence. Sadie and Theo Junior crossed the street, the lion padding behind them.

At the house, they saw the limousine parked out front.

"That's a stroke of luck," Theo Junior said. "Good old Grierson must have washed it. The garage will be empty."

"Here, hold this," Sadie said, and before he could protest, she handed him the end of the rope. Then she walked past the house and through the gate to the alley and hauled up the garage door.

It was large and clean inside. There were a couple of windows on the side, but they were too high up for anyone to look in. An old rug was rolled up at the back. Sadie laid it out.

"That ought to make a nice bed," she said. "And we can fill this bucket with water. But he needs a litter box. You don't have any sand, do you?"

"I think there are some bags up on the shelf. The chauffeur puts it on the drive in the winter."

"Good. We can dump some in the corner."

"What if he doesn't want to go in?"

"I thought of that." Sadie unslung her knapsack and took out a package of hotdogs. She opened the package and put them on the floor. The lion walked in and ate them in two bites.

"I guess he doesn't take mustard," Theo Junior said.

Sadie took off the collar.

"I know it will be boring in here. No dogs to chase, no peacocks to eat. But it's the best we can do for now. Goodnight, lion."

The animal stood watching as they stepped out and hauled down the door. They could hear him pacing a moment before lying down.

"Maybe the garage reminds him of his old circus cage," Theo Junior said.

"Then he hasn't had much of a life." Sadie took one more thing out of her knapsack — a lock. She put it through the iron loops on the door and the doorframe and locked it. Then she put the key on the string around her neck that held her house key.

"I'll tell Grierson that I'm doing a science project for school and that he should keep the car out of the garage because it might blow up," Theo Junior said.

"Sounds good. Now I'd better get home before my dad wakes up."

And with that she ran down the drive and disappeared into the dark.

10

_ ❋ _

The Search

Beast Hunt a Bust

Yesterday afternoon two vanloads of uniformed con-
stables disembarked on the north side of High Park
and lined up at attention. Each held a heavy wooden
club. Nearby gathered a less orderly crowd of fifty or
so men who had volunteered for the search. They carried hockey sticks, brooms and shovels.

Sergeant Jaworski, mounted on a noble steed,
trotted back and forth shouting directions through a
megaphone. He then blew a whistle, and the search
for the monster in the park commenced.

For three hours they combed the woods and
meadows.

The following interesting items were found: three pocket watches, a ukulele, one pair of long johns, and a very old bottle of Lyman's liver medicine with the cork still in it.

One group of volunteers encountered a displeased skunk, with unfortunate results. Also, a policeman temporarily detained Mrs. Emily Porterhouse, a local poet who was hanging pages of her verse in the trees.

Monsters, however, proved scarce.

A highly annoyed Sergeant Jaworski was seen pulling burrs off his trousers before galloping away. The crowd of volunteers dispersed.

Toronto, it seems, must remain just an ordinary city, without the fame of being home to a monster. At least for now.

11

※

Big Fists

THE NEXT DAY, Sadie visited the lion on her way to school.

Standing on a couple of wobbly milk crates, she could just see through the window at the back of the Kendricks' garage. The lion looked up when she told him she would be back later for a proper visit. Then she stayed in the alley while the chauffeur came out of the house to drive Theo Junior to school. Theo Junior attended the High Park Preparatory School for Boys, where he did not have a single friend.

The two of them met later, after Sadie had delivered her pies. Theo Junior brought the parcel of meat, and Sadie unlocked the garage door so they could slip inside.

By now the two felt no fear of the lion. At least, Sadie felt no fear, and Theo Junior was only slightly nervous. As for the lion, he was so impatient for supper that he nosed Sadie out of the way even as she was undoing the parcel.

As the lion ate, Theo Junior put fresh water from a hose into the bucket. Sadie went about the less pleasant task of cleaning the kitty litter.

"A big animal makes a big poop," she said, wrinkling her nose.

Then they kept the lion company for a while, talking quietly as he lay down and groomed himself. Sadie was happy just looking at him — at his deep eyes and beautiful face, the twitching whiskers and the lighter fur on his chin. He flicked his tail back and forth, the tuft at the end patting the ground.

But on the second day, the lion got up and walked around them in a circle, pacing along the walls.

"He's restless," she said. "I think he needs some exercise."

"Maybe we could get him to jump through a hoop," Theo Junior said. "That's what they do in the circus."

Sadie mulled over the idea, but she didn't like it. There was something, well, undignified about the idea of getting the lion to perform. Besides, he probably needed some fresh air, too.

"I'm going to come back tonight after dark," she said to Theo Junior. "Say, eleven o'clock. You can join me. Or not."

Of course, she knew that he would.

— • —

THAT NIGHT, Sadie put the collar and leash on the lion. Then she pulled up the garage door.

"Come on, lion," she said. "Walkies!"

The lion trotted behind as they went down the alley and turned onto another. A house cat stared at them from the top of a fence, as if unable to believe what it saw.

"You know, it's rather pleasant taking a walk with a lion at night," said Theo Junior. "I'm surprised more people don't do it."

They walked for almost an hour, always keeping behind the houses.

They were on their way back when Sadie said, "I went to the school library yesterday and read about lions. They live in Africa, usually in a group called a pride."

"Neat. Maybe the three of us could be a pride. We could even have our own chant, like a football team. *Who's got the best roar in town? We do! Who's got —*"

"I'm being serious, Theo Junior. Remember the first day you met him? You called him my lion. Sadie's lion — that's what you said. But I don't think a lion can belong to anybody. I think he should be in Africa."

They reached the alley behind Theo Junior's house. The lion walked into the garage without being asked and went to the bucket. He lapped up the water. Sadie took off the collar.

"Hey, you're splashing me! Okay, cutie, see you tomorrow."

They went out of the garage and Theo pulled down the door.

"How could we get him there?" he asked. "To Africa, I mean. It's thousands of miles away. Even if we had the money, we couldn't just buy him a ticket on a ship."

"So it isn't easy. But doesn't he deserve to go home?"

"I'll show you what you deserve," came a voice.

They turned. In the alley stood three dark figures. One was big and bulky, wearing a low cap. The other two were skinny.

The Parkside Gang.

"If it isn't the weirdest girl in the neighborhood," said Fergus Gumpy. "Who knew you had a rich friend?"

"Yeah, who knew?" said Dylan Tarpinsky.

"That's what I was going to say," said Wylie.

"My name is Theodore Kendrick Junior," said Theo. "And I'm pleased to make your acquaintance."

He put out his hand. Fergus smiled, took a step towards Theo Junior and punched him in the nose.

"Ahhg!" Theo Junior cried, his hands flying to his face. "You hit me!"

"Ain't you observant."

"Why don't you pick on someone your own size?" Sadie seethed.

"Do I have a nosebleed?"

"No, you're okay," she said, taking a look.

"I didn't even hit you hard, crybaby. You know what I deserve? I deserve to know what goodies you've got in that garage."

Sadie realized that she hadn't had a chance to lock it. "Oh, just a bunch of old furniture."

"We like smashing up junk," said Dylan.

"It's our hobby," said Wylie.

"We don't need to smash up junk when we can smash up these two," Fergus said. "Go on, boys. Hold their arms."

Before they knew what was happening, Sadie and Theo Junior each had their arms pinned behind them. Fergus spat in each hand and rubbed his palms together. Then he made two big fists.

"Hold 'em still."

"She's awfully squirmy," grunted Dylan.

"I better do her first, then."

Sadie wouldn't let herself turn away. She glared at Fergus. He cocked back his fist.

"Wait," Theo Junior blurted out. "There *is* something valuable in the garage."

Fergus held his fist in the air. "Like what?"

"Like … a fur coat."

"Theo, don't!" Sadie hissed.

"Is it in good condition?"

"Excellent condition. In fact, it still looks practically alive."

Fergus lowered his arm.

"All right, let's take a look. Maybe we can sell it to the pawnshop. Open the door and make it snappy."

"You can't, Theo!" Sadie said. She struggled but couldn't get out of Dylan's grip.

"Sorry, but I can't let them beat you up." Theo Junior bent down to grasp the handle of the garage door. With a groan he hauled it up.

Fergus Gumpy and the Tarpinsky twins heard a terrible sound. They saw a huge shape emerge from the blackness of the garage. A monster with shining eyes and enormous teeth.

Dylan Tarpinsky screamed. His brother Wylie screamed even louder. The two took off down the alley as fast as their skinny legs could carry them.

At first, Fergus just stared, his eyes wide and his mouth open. Then he, too, tried to run, only as he turned he tripped over his dangling shoelaces and landed flat on his face. The lion loomed over him and grabbed Fergus's jacket with his teeth.

He picked the boy up. It looked to Sadie and Theo Junior as if Fergus was swimming in the air, his arms and legs moving.

A low guttural sound came from the lion. He shook Fergus back and forth like he was a bag of laundry.

"Ah … ah … ah!"

The lion shook Fergus one last time and then tossed him into a group of garbage cans like a bowling ball hitting pins. The cans crashed over noisily as Fergus landed in a heap.

He didn't move.

Sadie and Theo Junior looked at one another.

Theo Junior whispered, "Is he…?"

A moan came from Fergus. They rushed over to help him up.

"Are you okay?" Sadie asked.

"You," he managed to say. "You … have … the monster!"

"No, you have it all wrong," Theo Junior said.

"I'm going … I'm going to tell …"

The lion roared.

It was a tremendous roar. Loud and terrible and also beautiful. It was a roar that seemed to make the air quiver. Fergus pushed Sadie and Theo Junior away even as he turned. He stumbled a few steps. Then he started to run as fast as he could down the alley.

Sadie and Fergus turned to the lion. He was look-ing at them and almost smiling, as if hoping for a hotdog.

"Thanks for saving us, lion," Sadie said. "But you shouldn't have done that."

The lion licked his whiskers. Then he turned and went back into the garage.

12

The Truth

It was after one o'clock in the morning by the time Sadie snuck back into the house and crept upstairs.

She got into her nightgown and crawled into bed. But she couldn't sleep.

Fergus Gumpy had seen the lion. In the dark he might not have been able to recognize what it was, but he sure knew that it was *something*. And Fergus was not the sort of person to keep that kind of news to himself.

Then there was the matter of what the lion did. He picked Fergus up. He shook him. He *threw* him. Yes, he was defending Sadie and Theo Junior. Maybe he did see them as his pride. But he hurt Fergus. He could have killed him.

Sadie didn't have any liking for Fergus Gumpy, but that didn't mean she wanted him dead. The lion wasn't just some enormous house cat. He was tremendously strong. He had teeth and claws. He was a natural predator. In his heart, he was *wild*. She couldn't just keep him like he was a pet. Maybe, deep down, that's what she had been trying to do.

But she couldn't keep him. Of course she couldn't.

— • —

THE FOLLOWING evening Sadie was just sitting down at the supper table when the doorbell rang. It made her jump in her seat.

"Now who would come to the door at this hour?" asked Miss Clemons. "It's simply uncouth. My own mother never tolerated it. She would throw a pan of dishwater out the window."

"Good idea," Sadie said, trying to sound calm. "I'll get the pan."

Theo Junior looked across the table at her. "Maybe you should get the door," he whispered.

"Oh, right." Sadie rose quickly from her chair.

"I'll go, too," Theo Junior said.

"It's probably for me," said Sadie's father, pushing back from the table.

76

"I'm certainly not going to be left behind," chirped Miss Clemons.

And so the four of them trooped to the front vestibule. When Mr. Menken opened the door, Sadie could see three policemen standing on the porch. And behind them was a grinning Fergus Gumpy. A small bandage was stuck to his forehead.

"Good evening, officers," her father said. "What brings you out? I hope we haven't broken any pie-baking laws, ha ha."

The officer in front made a harrumphing sound. "My name is Jaworski. Sergeant Jaworski. And there has been an accusation, sir. A very serious accusation. Harboring a dangerous animal."

"I don't understand."

"This young man, Mr. Ferguson Gumpy, who happens to be my nephew, has informed us that a vicious beast is being kept in the garage of a house nearby. The Kendricks' house. I don't like to disturb people of such quality but felt I had no choice, given the strange goings-on in this city. However, the owners of the house are out of town and the chauffeur would not let us look in the garage unless we had permission from the young master. And he told us where to find him."

Theo Junior began to tiptoe back inside. Sadie's father turned to him.

"Theodore Junior?"

"Yes?"

"Where are you going?"

"I didn't finish my spinach."

"Well, the spinach can wait. The sergeant here needs your assistance."

"That's right," said the officer. "If we could just walk back to the house and have a look in that garage."

"Of course we need to cooperate with the police," Miss Clemons said. "I have a file of clippings about people who did *not* cooperate. For example, there was the man in Newcastle who —"

"Very interesting, I'm sure," interrupted Sergeant Jaworski. "But I insist we stick to the purpose of this visit."

And so they went. Even Miss Clemons. They looked up at the impressive stone building behind the iron gate and the limousine parked on the drive.

"That's a big house," said Sadie's father. "Do you have a lot of brothers and sisters, Theo Junior?"

"Nope, there's just me. And of course the cook and the maid and good old Grierson."

The chauffeur was standing at the front door.

"I'm sorry to bother you with this unnecessary matter, Theo Junior."

"That's all right, Grierson."

"Enough chitchat," grumbled Sergeant Jaworski. "The garage is around the back."

He marched on and the others followed. Theo Junior turned to Sadie.

"What are we going to do?"

But at that moment, Fergus came up to them.

"I hope you're both going to like the Don Jail. I hear the gruel is delicious, and the bugs give it a nice crunch."

"All right, let's get on with it," the sergeant said. "Do you give me permission or not, boy?"

"Hmm." Theo Junior rubbed his chin. "That's a good question."

"I think you'd better," said Mr. Menken.

Sadie pressed something into Theo Junior's hand. It was the key for the lock.

"Go ahead," she said.

Theo Junior stared at Sadie. He tried to hide the key in his pocket, but he dropped it instead.

"Go on," said Sergeant Jaworski.

Theo Junior took off the lock. As soon as he did, the other two policemen stepped forward and grabbed the handle on the garage door. Sergeant Jaworski turned on a powerful flashlight.

The door lifted up.

Light filled the garage.

Nothing.

The garage was empty but for a rug and a pile of sand.

Theo Junior had been holding his breath. He let out such a sigh that he practically fainted. Then he looked at Sadie.

She shrugged.

Sergeant Jaworski stepped into the garage. He sniffed loudly.

"It smells in here," he said. "It smells of animal."

"That's very observant," Theo Junior said quickly. "I used to keep a pair of guinea pigs in a cage. I named them Fred and Adele after the famous dancers. Actually, they looked more like furry slippers with eyes. Sometimes I put little hats on them, and I tried to teach them tricks like roll over and beg, but all they really wanted to do was eat and make little poops. And then Fred ate his hat and died. Or maybe it was Adele. I couldn't tell —"

"I'm not talking about any guinea pigs!" Sergeant Jaworski burst out, his face red. He took off his cap and ran his hand through his hair.

"It seems we were given wrong information. Forgive us for interrupting your supper hour. Now you, Ferguson, come with me."

"But, Uncle, I swear it's true!"

Sergeant Jaworski grabbed Fergus by the collar and pulled him away.

— • —

SADIE, HER FATHER, Theo Junior and Miss Clemons headed back to their now-cold supper.

Theo Junior hissed into Sadie's ear. "You moved the ... you-know-what? And you didn't tell me?"

"Last night, after you left, I took him back to the hollow. I decided we couldn't leave him in the garage. I was going to tell you."

"I thought we were going to jail. I thought I was going to have to eat crunchy gruel."

"But I'm still worried. It's not safe in the park anymore, either. I don't know what to do."

Later that evening, Sadie was in her room trying to concentrate on her homework. A tap sounded on the door.

"Can I come in?" came her father's voice.

"Sure."

He closed the door behind him.

"I think we need to clear things up, Sadie."

"Clear what up?"

"Exactly what's going on. Theo Junior is a nice boy and I'm glad you've made a friend. But something smells fishy. Yesterday I woke up in the night because I heard the front door open. I heard you go into your room. And now we have the police at the door. I'm not angry but I am a little disappointed that you would keep secrets from me. Even more than that, I'm worried. And I will be angry if you lie to me. Do you understand?"

"Yes, Dad."

"Are you in trouble, Sadie?"

Sadie sat up. "No. Maybe. I'm not sure. Yes."

"Tell me."

She was silent for a long minute.

"It's pretty hard to explain. I think the best way is to show you. But you'll have to come with me."

"Where?"

"Into the park."

"Let's go, then."

It was getting dark, and cool. They walked to the east gate of the park. They didn't talk as Sadie led her father off the path and through the trees to the clearing.

The moon was starting to wane. A soft light filled the clearing, dappled by the shadows of surrounding leaves. The tree's tangle of roots looked like snakes. The hollow below was absolutely black.

"Was that tree struck by lightning? I hope you weren't out here when it happened," her father said.

"No, it's not about the tree. It's in there. That hollow." Sadie pointed.

Her father stepped forward and bent down to peer in. Sadie grabbed his arm and pulled him back.

"You'd better not get too close. He doesn't know you."

"He?"

"Let me show you." She stepped up. "Hey, there. Do you want to come out and meet my dad?"

"Who's in there, Sadie?"

She put a finger to her lips.

The two yellow eyes appeared in the hollow. Sadie called again. The eyes grew larger and the lion emerged from the dark.

Her father reached out to grab her arm and pulled them both backwards.

"I don't believe it."

The lion yawned, showing his teeth, and then flopped down, beating his tail on the ground.

"You really *are* hiding a beast. Isn't he dangerous?"

"Not to people who are nice to him. Theo Junior and I have been bringing him food. I hope you don't mind. I used up a package of baloney today."

"Was he actually in the Kendricks' garage?"

"Just for a little while. So the police wouldn't find him when they searched the park. I'm trying to keep him safe, Dad. But now I don't know what to do."

"No," said her father, stepping forward to take her hand. "I don't suppose you do. The question is, do I?"

13

— ✳ —

Research

SADIE'S FATHER promised not to do anything until the morning. Still, she had a restless night and was glad to get up for breakfast. In the kitchen, her father was kneading dough for the next batch of pies.

"He's an incredible animal," her father said, sprinkling flour on the counter top. "I've never seen anything so magnificent. But someone might get hurt. It's a wonder nobody has up to now, including you and Theo Junior."

"I know," Sadie said. "I didn't realize it at first but I do now."

"I've no choice but to tell the police. People have to come first."

"But why?" asked Sadie. "Why is a person more important than an animal?"

Her father scratched his nose, dusting it with flour. "That's a good question. I could give you several reasons but I'm not sure that you'd be convinced by them. And we still have to do something before a tragedy occurs."

"It's not fair. I'm the one who told you about the lion. Why do you get to decide?"

"Because I'm the grown-up. And please lower your voice."

"I never should have told you!"

"Now, Sadie —"

A knock sounded on the kitchen door. It swung open to reveal Miss Clemons, her reading glasses dangling on a cord around her neck.

"I am sorry to barge in," she said. "But I heard raised voices. I think of you as my family and I can't stand by while there is discord in this house. Perhaps I can help."

"That's very kind of you, Miss Clemons," said Sadie's father. "But I don't believe there's anything you can do."

"Yes, there is," Sadie said. "You can give us your opinion, Miss Clemons. It's about something I found."

"Found?"

"It was lost during a train accident."

"A train accident, you say? Far more common than people realize. I remember the two Eastern Railway freight trains that collided in Yorkshire. The Norwegian train disaster near Trondheim. And let's not forget the Winslow Junction derailment in New Jersey …"

"This one was a bit closer to home. And it was a few weeks ago."

"Did I not read a newspaper report about just such an accident? A circus train, if I recall."

"That's the one," Sadie said. "Something … fell out of the train and I found it. Dad wants to give it to, well, to the authorities. But I don't want to."

"Perhaps I can help. Librarians always begin by asking questions. Do you wish to keep it?"

Sadie thought. "I know that I can't."

"Then who do *you* want to give it to?"

Miss Clemons really was good at asking questions. Sadie thought again, but this time for longer. At last she said, "I want to give it back to the person it belongs to."

"Very well," said Miss Clemons. "After questions comes the search for information. Information is crucial. We need to know more about this train, and that takes research. Fortunately, I believe I kept that newspaper clipping."

"You did?" Sadie and her father said at the same time.

"But what subject did I file it under? *Reasons Not to Travel? Mishaps in the Entertainment Field?* I'm sure I can find it in two shakes of a lamb's tail."

Miss Clemons went up the stairs to her room. Sadie's father went back to rolling his dough, and Sadie began to lay out the pie plates.

It was only a few minutes before they heard a cry of "Victory!"

Moments later, Miss Clemons bustled into the room. She put on her reading glasses.

"Ah, here it is. In the second paragraph. Wasserman's circus."

"Now what?" asked Sadie's father.

"We need to know where the office of the circus is located. You see, every circus has a headquarters. The article doesn't say where it is. However, there is a photograph of the train from before the accident. It says something on the side but I can't make it out. Fortunately, I always keep my trusty aid nearby for just such an occasion."

Miss Clemons fished in the side pocket of her dress and came up with a silver-handled magnifying glass.

"Sadie, your young eyes are no doubt the sharpest. See if you can make it out."

Sadie took the magnifying glass and held it up to the photograph in the clipping.

"I think I can," she said. "*Wasserman's Spectacular*

Circus and Animal Menagerie. And under that it says, *Pensacola, Florida.*"

"Very good, Sadie," said Miss Clemons. "And now what do we do?"

"We call them on the telephone!" Sadie practically shouted. "Oh, Miss Clemons! You're a genius!"

"I am not a genius," said Miss Clemons with a smile. "I am a librarian. Which, I would venture to say, is almost as good."

— • —

Miss Clemons went to meet her friend Abigail Foster at the Parkview Tea Room, as she did every day. Sadie and her father went to the telephone in the hall.

"We've never made a long-distance call before," Sadie said.

"There's a first time for everything." Her father picked up the earpiece and dialed zero. "Hello, Operator? I'd like to place a call to Wasserman's Spectacular Circus and Animal Menagerie in Pensacola, Florida. No, I don't know the number. Thank you."

Sadie stood watching her father as he waited. One minute went by, then another. Sadie tapped her foot nervously. What was taking so long?

"Hello? Wasserman circus? I'd like to speak to the animal trainer. You say he's traveling with the circus?

Cincinnati, Ohio? Perhaps there's a number where I can reach him. No? Then can you give him my number? It's Roger 3108. Tell him we've got something of his. No, this isn't a joke."

Her father hung up.

"What happens now?" Sadie asked.

"The circus manager on the train calls the office every day when they arrive in a new town. He should be calling in the next two hours. You're already late for school so you might as well stay home. Besides, it will be nice to have your company in the kitchen. I've already fallen behind."

So Sadie and her father rolled out the pastry and pressed it into the pie plates. They added the filling. They pinched on the top crust, made crosshatches to let out the steam and slipped the pies into the oven. The Lake Simcoe ice wagon stopped at the house and her father loaded new blocks into the two ice boxes.

It felt strange to Sadie that regular life still had to continue, that her father had to fill his orders and that people had to eat their pie.

The telephone rang. Sadie froze.

"Answer it, Sadie."

"But I'm a kid!"

"You're the kid who found the lion. Quick now."

She sprinted to the hall and picked up the earpiece. "Hello?"

"This is Sam Hibbins calling," came a voice that

sounded as if it was from the other end of a tunnel. "I'm the assistant animal trainer of the Wasserman circus. You left a message? About finding something? I've got a lot of hungry animals waiting to be fed."

Sadie took a breath. "My name is Sadie Menken and I live in Toronto. I think you left behind a lion."

There was a long pause. "Our lion was killed in a train accident."

"The lion is living in High Park, right up from where the accident happened."

"Sunshine is alive? I can't believe it! I looked for him for as long as I could but then I had to rejoin the circus. The company said he was dead. I can't tell you how glad I am. Good old Sunny."

"His name is Sunny?"

"Sunshine. That's what I always called him, because of his sunny disposition. A real sweetie pie."

"He sure is."

"So you've actually seen him? He's all right?"

"We've been feeding him and trying to keep him safe, me and my friend Theo Junior. But the police have been looking for him, and I'm afraid —"

"I can be in Toronto in two days. Can you keep him safe until then?"

"We'll do everything we can. But hurry."

"I will. And I'll telephone again when I'm close so we can arrange to meet."

"Mr. Hibbins?"

"Yes, Sadie?"

"Did Sunshine like being in the circus? I mean, was he happy there? Will he be glad to go back?"

"Let's talk about that when I get to Toronto."

The line went dead.

14

Sam Hibbins

WAITING FOR Sam Hibbins felt like the longest two days Sadie had ever lived.

She and Theo Junior took the lion his evening meal, accompanied by her father.

"I shouldn't let you do this at all," he said. "But I certainly can't let you do it alone." He added an extra serving of ground beef to make sure the lion wouldn't be hungry, and he made them go right back home.

The next evening the telephone rang just after dinner. Sadie and Theo Junior hurried into the hall to find her father talking to Sam Hibbins, who had stopped at a diner several miles outside of town. They arranged to meet at the east gate of the park at midnight.

Mr. Menken insisted on sending Theo Junior home.

"The two of you have done enough for this creature," he said. "I'll take care of it."

Sadie did not sleep for a second. For days and days she had gone to sleep thinking about the lion. In the mornings he was the first thing on her mind. During school she worried, but just the thought of him lying in his hollow made her happy. And the best part of every day came after the lion had finished his meal. She remembered how he flopped down beside her. Sometimes, when he leaned against her, she could feel the slow rise and fall of his breathing.

But that would soon be over.

When the grandfather clock in the hall chimed to mark half past eleven, she got up and dressed. She sat on her bed and waited until she heard her father in the front hall.

"Sadie?" he said, turning to her.

"Dad, I just have to come."

"All right, then. Let's go."

They went out the door and her father locked it behind them. A sudden rustling sound made them both freeze on the porch.

Theo Junior emerged from the bushes.

"I should have known," her father said.

The three of them walked to the park. They stood in the dark for just a few minutes before an old Model T truck wheezed down the road and stopped beside them. On the side were the words *Wasserman's Spectacular Circus and Animal Menagerie*, the paint all chipped.

The engine coughed, sputtered and died. Sadie could see a man in the front seat with a small dog beside him.

"Stay in the truck, Daisy," said the man as he got out. He was short and round and wore a battered straw hat. He walked with a limp.

"Which one of you is Sadie Menken?"

"I am," said Sadie.

"I was joking. Of course it's you. And a girl with plenty of moxie, you are, taking care of Sunshine. Let me shake your hand, and yours, too, Mr. Menken. And while I'm at it, let me have yours, young fellow."

"I'm Theodore Kendrick Junior and I'm very glad to meet you. Did you get that limp in the train crash?"

"No, that was given to me by a Bengal tiger in the ring. Tigers are very hard to work with. Give me a lion every time. Shall we go and get Sunny?"

Sadie looked up into Sam Hibbins' face. "I would like you to answer my question first. About whether Sunshine will be happy going back to the circus."

"Fair enough," said the man. "Sunny never liked being in the circus much. The crowds made him nervous. He didn't like all the noise and lights. He wouldn't perform. In truth, Mr. Wasserman was getting good and sick of Sunny."

Sadie shook her head. "I've changed my mind. I don't think Sunny should go back to the circus. I think he ought to go back to Africa. He should live where lions are supposed to live."

Sam Hibbins smiled a little. He pulled a straw from his hat and used it to scratch behind his ear.

"That's sure a nice idea, Sadie. Putting Sunshine on the African savannah along with the elephants and zebras. Letting him join a pride and hunt and make babies and lie in the warm sun."

"Exactly!"

"The problem is that Sunny wasn't born in Africa. He was born in our headquarters in Florida. His mother rejected him so I raised the little cub myself. Fed him with a bottle. Played with him. He's lived in captivity his whole life. He'd never survive in the wild. He wouldn't know how to protect himself, or join the other lions, or hunt."

"He ate some dogs," said Theo Junior.

"Catching a speeding antelope is something else altogether. In Africa he would die of shock, or starvation, or get mauled by other lions. Maybe it isn't right for wild animals to be trained for the circus. After forty years in the business, I'm starting to think so. But it's too late for Sunny."

Sadie felt tears rising. "I was hoping he'd have a happy ending."

Her father put his hand on her shoulder. "Mr.

Hibbins, is there any way to give the poor fellow a better life?"

"I've been thinking about that my whole way here. You see, I'm about ready to retire. I'm getting old and, besides, I've lost my taste for it. I've got a nice piece of property in Florida. Five acres of fenced-in land. If I can get Mr. Wasserman to sell Sunny to me, I'll take him there. He can have regular meals and bask in the sunshine. He'll be retired, too. I think that's the best we can hope for. It would be an *all right* ending, anyway. What do you say, Sadie?"

Sadie looked over at Theo Junior. He nodded. She looked at her father and then at Sam.

"Okay," she said.

"Then let's go get him."

Sam went back to his truck and took out a leash and collar that weren't much different from the ones Sadie had used. He also took out a wooden club.

"What's that for?" Sadie said with alarm.

"Don't you worry. I never use this. But even the tamest lion can be dangerous. It doesn't hurt to have something to wave about. You've been lucky, and of course Sunny has come to like you. But if a lion becomes surprised or scared or mad, he might do something aggressive just by instinct. Now, you lead the way, Sadie, and I'll follow."

Sadie felt that Sam Hibbins was a man to trust. So she led him into the park, along the path and through the trees. She was so used to the way that she didn't stumble once.

They stood looking at the dark hollow.

"In there?" Sam asked.

"Uh-huh."

He took a step forward.

"Hey, Sunshine," he crooned. "Hey, pal, it's old Sam. Come and say hello to your buddy."

Sadie did not expect what happened next.

The lion charged out of the dark. She almost screamed, afraid for the trainer and the lion both. But instead, Sam laughed as the huge animal landed its big paws on his shoulders, almost knocking him off his feet, and began to lick his face.

"Come on now, Sunny. I don't need a bath."

"Gee whiz," whistled Theo Junior. "Does he ever remember you!"

"He looks good. You've been feeding him well. Get off me, you big lug! That's better. Now, see? You've knocked off my hat. You have to remember, Sadie, that I fed him when he was a little thing. He thinks I'm his mother. But I'm the only person he hasn't been afraid of until now, so he must really like you folks."

His words made Sadie feel better. The sight of the lion so happy to see Sam had made her a little jealous. She watched as the trainer put on the collar and gave Sunshine a rub on the head.

"Time to go, Sunny."

Sam kept the leash short and the club in his other hand as he walked behind the others, always keeping an eye on the lion. When they got to the truck, he took off the collar, opened up the back and pulled down a plank. Sadie saw a bed of straw inside. Sunshine walked straight up, swishing his tail.

He didn't even look back.

Sam closed up the truck.

"I never thought I'd see Sunny again." His eyes shone. "He's always been my favorite."

Sadie couldn't hold back her own tears now. "I'm going to miss him so much. Will you let us know what happens to him?"

"I promise. Sunny owes you a lot. His life, probably. And I owe you, too."

Once more he shook Sadie's hand, then Theo Junior's, and then Mr. Menken's. He climbed into the truck and this time got jumped on by the little dachshund.

"Her name is Daisy?" Sadie said.

"That's right. She's a good little thing."

"Maybe you'd better keep her away from Sunshine. He might have developed a taste for dogs."

Sam touched two fingers to his hat and then started the wheezy engine.

Mr. Menken put an arm around Sadie's shoulder and another around Theo Junior. They watched

Sam wave out the window as the truck puttered away.

Sadie sniffled a little. She thought the moment called for something grand or poetic, but she couldn't think of anything.

"Goodbye, lion," she said.

15

— ✳ —

The Rest of the Story

WASSERMAN'S SPECTACULAR Circus and Animal Menagerie never reported the fact that they had lost a lion. Nor was the mystery of the disappearing dogs, the demise of a peacock, or the appearance of a monstrous beast in a Toronto park ever solved.

In the last week of June, workers sawed the lightning-blasted tree into pieces and carted them away. They filled in the hollow with new soil. By late July, the mound was already overgrown with grass and wild bluebells.

And anyone who looked closely could have seen a pale and tiny maple sapling starting to uncurl a single leaf. Over the decades it would grow into a broad and leafy giant.

Sam Hibbins drove his truck at a slow and steady pace, stopping from time to time for coffee and sandwiches — accompanied by a dozen hamburgers, rare. He caught up to the circus in St. Louis, Missouri, and went immediately to speak to Mr. Wasserman in his private train car.

Considering that Mr. Wasserman thought Sunny to be nothing but a nuisance, the owner was surprisingly stubborn about selling him. As Sam wrote to Sadie, *Mr. Wasserman insists that I try to bring Sunny into the ring one more time. I'm going to spend a week training him and then we'll just have to see how he does.*

Did Sam really try his best to train Sunny? The lion's appearance in the ring was a complete failure.

Sunny will just never be a good circus lion, Sam wrote to Sadie. *Even Mr. Wasserman agrees. He still wouldn't sell Sunny to me. Instead, he gave him to me! But he did make me pay for the truck, which I need to transport the dear fellow to his retirement home.*

That news caused Sadie to whoop for joy. As did the letters over the next few weeks that described how much the lion liked exploring his five acres. He would roll in the dust, sleep in the sun when it was cool and in the shade when it was hot. Sam Hibbins walked the grounds every day and the lion often followed.

Six months later, Sam wrote that he had decided to stop entering the grounds where the lion now lived.

Sunny has gotten bigger and heavier. Now that he has some space to roam and feels more like himself, I'm worried that he might suddenly remember he's a lion. I'm sure he'd feel awful if he hurt me. Besides, who would take care of him?

But then Sam wrote to say that one day Daisy slipped under the gate into the field. She headed straight for the lion. Sunshine greeted the dog by licking her snout, and the two curled up together in the sun.

I can't seem to keep Daisy out of there, Sam wrote. *So I've given up. I just let her spend every day with Sunshine.*

Sadie and Theo Junior remained friends. In 1929 the stock-market crash began the Great Depression, and the Kendrick family lost its fortune. Theo Junior's parents had to sell the house and limousine and move across the country to Prince George, British Columbia, to live with an uncle. Theo Junior eventually became a high-school teacher and was very popular with the students. He was known for his jaunty bow ties and checkered blazers.

The Depression was hard on Sadie and her father, too. But they survived because in hard times, people's spirits could always be lifted by a good piece of pie. And the household took in another boarder. Abigail

Foster, Miss Clemons' friend, proved to be an equally good conversationalist at the supper table.

Sadie became one of the few women veterinarians of her time. She took care of countless dogs, cats, birds, rabbits, snakes and other animals. Her own house became a kind of menagerie of creatures that had been mistreated. There were always two or three dogs, an equal number of cats, and perhaps a turtle or rabbit.

Sadie had one son, and it was to this boy that she told the story of the lion in High Park. When the boy became a man and had a family of his own, he told the story to his own three children.

One of those children — the youngest — was me.

That means that Sadie Menken was my grandmother.

Sadie and Sam continued to write to one another for a long time. Many years later, most of the letters were lost when Sadie grew old and moved east to Prince Edward Island, into a little house by the sea. When I was small I would walk with her in her garden, followed by dogs and cats, and ask her about the lion. And she would always say the same thing.

"Oh, I remember Sunny as if it were yesterday."

My grandmother is gone now, but I keep a photograph of her as a young woman on my desk. She is sitting on a wooden chair on the lawn of a small house. There are four dogs sitting at her feet and a fat cat purring in her lap (at least, I imagine it is purring). A parrot sits on her shoulder, poking at her earring.

The photograph is very precious to me. As is the story that she told me, about how, a long time ago, a lion escaped from a train and lived in a park, and was found by a girl named Sadie Menken, and had an all-right ending.

Acknowledgments

I am honored to have made many books with the late Sheila Barry. She was the finest of editors and the warmest of people, and I am just one of the many writers who will miss her.

My gratitude to Shelley Tanaka for her fine editing skills and for finding the right title. Also to Nan Froman, Michael Solomon, Nolan Pelletier for the cover illustration, and everyone at Groundwood. Thanks to Rachel Fagan for reading the proofs and making some late catches.

Finally, I want to thank my mother and father for having taken me to the wondrous High Park when I was a child, where we fished in Grenadier Pond, picnicked under the trees and chased the peacocks.

CARY FAGAN has won the Vicky Metcalf Award, the Jewish Book Award and the IODE Jean Throop Book Award, and his books have been nominated for the Rogers Writers' Trust Fiction Prize, the Giller Prize, the Silver Birch Award, the Norma Fleck Award and the Rocky Mountain Book Award. He is the author of several popular short novels and picture books, including *Danny, Who Fell in a Hole* and *A Cage Went in Search of a Bird* (illustrated by Banafsheh Erfanian). His stories are often set in Toronto, Cary's hometown.